THE
SELKIE GIRL

RETOLD BY SUSAN COOPER

ILLUSTRATED BY WARWICK HUTTON

A MARGARET K. McELDERRY BOOK

NEW YORK

This book is for Margaret

ALSO BY SUSAN COOPER AND WARWICK HUTTON
The Silver Cow: A Welsh Tale
A Margaret K. McElderry Book

Margaret K. McElderry Books
Macmillan Publishing Company
866 Third Avenue
New York, NY 10022
Collier Macmillan Canada, Inc.
Manufactured by Dai Nippon Manufacturing Company in Japan
10 9 8 7 6 5 4 3 2
ISBN 0-689-50390-3
Library of Congress Catalog Card Number: 86-70147
First Edition

The islands rise green out of the sea, where the waves foam over the grey rocks, and strange things may happen there.

Donallan lived on the biggest island. He had a small farmhouse called a croft, with ten sheep grazing a few acres of land, and he had a boat for fishing in the sea. His parents were dead and he had no wife, so he lived there, with only a dog called Angus, to herd the sheep, and a cat called Cat to keep the croft free of mice. He was lonely, sometimes. He would listen to the wind singing in the chimney, and wish it were a human voice.

One spring morning Donallan went down to the beach, with his dog Angus for company, to rake up the seaweed that he dug into his garden each year. He had gathered a great bale of weed when he thought he heard music, from the rocks beside the sea. It was like the voice of the wind, but Donallan was a long way from his chimney. He went to look, and in wonder and delight he saw three beautiful girls sitting on the rocks, naked, combing their long hair.

One of the girls had fair hair, one red, and one black.
The fair-haired girl was singing. She was the most beautiful of
the three, and Donallan could not take his eyes from her. He
gazed and gazed at her gleaming white body and her long-
lashed dark eyes, and he listened to her lilting voice singing its
wordless song. And he knew suddenly that he would never be
happy unless he could share his life with this magical girl.

Then Angus the dog turned from chasing a crab and saw the girls, and he began to growl deep in his throat, like summer thunder far away. The three girls looked up, startled, and saw Donallan and his dog. In an instant each of them snatched up a shapeless bundle that was lying at her side, and plunged over the edge of the rocks into the sea. And all at once they were no longer girls but selkies, grey seals, three sleek shapes flashing dark through the waves.

Donallan stood on the beach, forlorn. "Come back!" he called to his memory of the lovely singing girl. "Oh, come back!"

But nothing was there but the empty sea.

Donallan went sadly home, carrying his bale of seaweed, and on the way he met Old Thomas. Thomas was the most ancient man in the islands; he had a lame leg, and only three teeth left in his head, but he had sharp eyes. "And what is the matter with you, Donallan?" he said. "Did the sea take your boat in exchange for that fine weed?"

Donallan sighed. "I am in love," he said, and he told Old Thomas about the beautiful vanished girls who had turned into seals.

"Oh dear me," said Old Thomas, whistling through his three teeth. "A bad choice you have made. For those are the daughters of the King of Lochlann, out beyond the sea's brim, and they are selkies indeed. Just once a year, on the seventh day of the highest tides of spring, they get the land-longing on them, and they slip out of their skins and take human form for a day."

"I love her, the fair-haired one," Donallan said. "I want her to be my wife."

"There's only one way for that," Old Thomas said.

"What is it then?" said Donallan quickly. "Tell me, tell me!"

Old Thomas looked thoughtfully at Donallan's bale of
seaweed. "And what will you give me if I tell you?" he said.

"This fine weed for your garden," Donallan said. "And
one like it every year."

"Will you carry it to my croft?"

"I will," Donallan said eagerly.

"And will you dig it into the soil?"

"I will, I will!" Donallan snatched Old Thomas up from
the ground, perched him on top of the seaweed and carried
him off towards his croft. *"Tell me!"* he said.

Old Thomas grinned down at him. "You must wait until this same day next year," he said, "at the seventh stream of the flood tide in spring. And if then you are still foolish enough to be in love, you must go to that rock and steal the bundle that is beside the selkie girl, when she is out of the sea. For that is her skin, and without it she cannot become a seal again. You must not destroy it, or she will die, but as long as you keep it safe and hidden, she will follow you and stay with you."

Donallan shouted for joy.

Old Thomas said quietly, "But a wild creature will always go back to the wild, in the end."

Donallan paid no heed to that. He waited for a year, then
went back to the rocky beach on the seventh day of the spring
flood tides. There were the three girls again, the fair-haired one
singing even more bewitchingly than before. Donallan crept
up to the rock where they sat. The dark-haired girl caught
sight of him and cried out in warning, and all three girls dived
at once into the sea—but Donallan had hold of the bundled
sealskin of the girl he loved.

She begged him from the waves, "Oh please, give me
back my skin!"

Out in the ocean swells, Donallan could see two gleaming
shapes swimming, waiting for her: a dark grey seal, and one
with a reddish skin.

"Come with me!" he called to the selkie girl. "Come with me and be my wife, and I will work for you and love you well, and we shall be happy all our days!" He walked away up the beach with her skin, knowing she must follow, and when she came after him he gave her a soft woollen shawl that had belonged to his mother, to cover her nakedness. She was crying bitterly, but she followed him.

So Donallan married the selkie girl, and they lived
together in the croft with the dog and the cat, and the sheep
outside grazing the hills. She would not tell him her true name,
so he called her Mairi. He kept her sealskin hidden, checking it
often to make sure it never cracked or dried out. After the
first day, she never asked for it again.

Mairi worked as hard as Donallan on the croft, and because he was gentle and loving, she no longer wept. When their first child was born, he saw her smile. But he never heard her sing again, and each year when the seventh day of the flood tides came round, in the spring, he would find her looking sadly out at the sea, with her head tilted as if she were listening.

As the years passed, five children were born to Mairi and Donallan: three boys and two girls. They were called Dougal, Margaret, Niall, Kate Annie and James. They were bright, handsome children, sweet-voiced and strong-backed, and they lived happily on the croft by the sea. Only Kate Annie, who was thoughtful, wondered why she felt sometimes that her quiet mother had lost something precious, and wished that she could give it back to her again.

One summer day, Donallan got up very early before the sunrise, because it was his day for checking secretly that the sealskin was safe and well. Softly he went outside and he pulled three stones from the wall of the house, which was as thick as a man's arm is long. Then he took out the sealskin, spread it flat on the ground, rubbed it carefully with oil and put it back again. He did not see his youngest son James, who had come creeping out of the house after him. James stared. What was his father doing, so secret, so early in the morning? He slipped back indoors to his bed, wondering. What was so special about the skin of a seal?

Later that day, Donallan took the three biggest children
out to the fields. James went outside the house and looked at
the wall. He could see the place where his father had moved the
stones. He went back to his mother, who was making oatcakes
with Kate Annie.

"Mother," he said, "why is my father keeping an old
sealskin in our wall?"

Mairi stopped mixing the dough. Very slowly she put
down the bowl and spoon on the table, and she looked at
James as if she had never seen him before. Both children saw
a glow of happiness like sunlight in her face, and for the first
time in their lives they heard her laugh.

"Oh, James!" she said. "You have found my skin!"

She took his hand, and Kate Annie's, and the three of them
ran outside and took the sealskin from the wall. Mairi laughed
again in delight, and Kate Annie felt warm at the sound.

"Come," Mairi said to them, and with the skin in her arms she led them down to the sea. Kate Annie felt frightened, and yet she knew that something right was happening, whatever it might be.

Their mother said to them, "Be brave, because I must leave you. For I was brought here from my own people against my will, twenty years past, and I have five children in the sea and five on the land. And that is a hard case to be in."

Kate Annie said, "We have brothers and sisters in the sea?"

"You have," she said, "and so do I."

"Don't go," James said. He blinked hard, because he felt he was too old to cry.

"I love you," Mairi said, and she stroked his hair. "I shall never be far away." She raised her head, and looked out at the sea.

"You must go to them. It's their turn," Kate Annie said. She took her brother's hand. "I'll look after James."

Mairi stepped into the sea, and smiled at the wash of the waves about her feet. She said, "I shall always be here, watching over you, whether you are in the islands or on the sea. I promise you. And every year, at the seventh stream of the flood tide in spring, you will all see me as I am now."

She kissed them and she dived into the sea, holding the sealskin. Out in the ocean swells they saw two gleaming shapes

swimming, waiting for her: a dark grey seal, and one with a reddish skin. Then suddenly there were three, as a light-coloured seal joined them. The three curved and swirled and dived together in the foaming water—and then they were gone.

"She isn't drowned, is she?" James said.

"Of course not," said Kate Annie. "Come home and we'll bake the oatcakes."